The RUNAWAY PANCAKE

Retold by Mairi Mackinnon

Illustrated by
Silvia Provantini

There was once a family
with seven children, and
they were always hungry.

3

One day, their mother decided to make pancakes for breakfast.

First she mixed
flour, eggs and milk.

Then she poured the mix into a pan to cook. She tossed the first pancake, up in the air and down again.

Almost ready now.

But the pancake
didn't want to be
eaten. It jumped
right out of the pan and
rolled out of the door.

7

"Come back!" called the children and they all went running after it.

The pancake rolled out of the gate and into the road, faster and faster.

The dog was snoozing in his kennel when the pancake rolled past.

Mmm, a pancake!

"You look good,"
he barked.

"Come here
and let me taste you."

"No!" said the pancake and rolled on, with the dog and all the family chasing behind.

A rabbit in a field saw
the pancake rolling past.

"How fast you roll!" he said. "Can I catch you?"

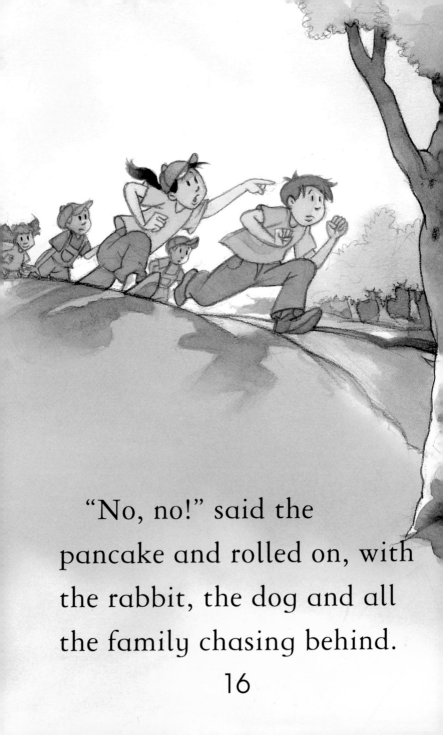

"No, no!" said the
pancake and rolled on, with
the rabbit, the dog and all
the family chasing behind.

16

17

A duck on the stream saw the pancake rolling past.

A pancake!
How tasty!

"Stop, Mr. Pancake!" she called. "Just let me try a tiny piece of you."

"No, no, no!" said the
pancake and rolled on,
with the duck, the rabbit,

the dog and all the family chasing behind.

Faster, faster!

A cat in the farmyard
saw the pancake roll past.

Is it a game?

"Stop! Wait for me!"
she called.

"Catch me if you can,"
said the pancake and rolled
on, with the cat, the duck,
the rabbit, the dog and all
the family chasing behind.

24

A goat in a meadow saw
the pancake roll past.

Mmm,
delicious!

"What a
fine-looking
        pancake," he said.
        "Do you taste as good
            as you look?"

27

"Of course!" said the
pancake and rolled on...

with the goat, the cat,
the duck, the rabbit, the
dog and all the family
chasing behind.

But you're not
tasting me!

A fox in some bushes saw
the pancake rolling past.

"Oh, Mr. Pancake," he
said. "Why is everyone
    chasing you? What
       have you done?"

"Can't stop
now," said the pancake...

and it hitched a ride
on a kite to escape the fox.

It landed at the edge
of a forest. By the forest
was a pig in a pen.

Now the pig wanted to eat the pancake too, but he was too clever to say so.

35

"What's the hurry, Mr. Pancake?" he asked. "Let me walk through the forest with you. It's a dangerous place."

The pancake looked into
the forest. Maybe the pig
was right.

"Quickly!" he gasped. "Don't let them catch me!"

"What did
you say?" asked
the pig.

"I SAID, DON'T LET THEM CATCH ME!" shouted the pancake.

"Who?"
asked the pig.
"THEM!" said
the pancake.

42

"I'm sorry," said the pig. "I can't hear you. You'll have to come closer."

The pancake jumped over
the fence and into the pen.

"I SAID, THE FOX, THE GOAT," the pancake began. But before he could shout any more, the pig snapped him up and swallowed him...

...in one gulp.

About the story

The Runaway Pancake is a folk tale from Germany and Norway. There are different versions with different characters, but the pancake always gets eaten at the end.

Designed by Louise Flutter
Series designer: Russell Punter
Series editor: Lesley Sims

This edition first published in 2013 by Usborne Publishing Ltd., Usborne House, 83-85 Saffron Hill, London EC1N 8RT, England. www.usborne.com Copyright © 2013, 2006 Usborne Publishing Ltd.